The REAL STORY OF STONE SOUP

BY

Ying Chang Compestine

ILLUSTRATED BY

Stéphane Jorisch

DUTTON CHILDREN'S BOOKS

DUTTON CHILDREN'S BOOKS

A division of Penguin Young Readers Group

PUBLISHED BY THE PENGUIN GROUP

Penguin Group (USA) Inc., 375 Hudson Street, New York, New York 10014, U.S.A. /
Penguin Group (Canada), 90 Eglinton Avenue East, Suite 700, Toronto, Ontario, Canada M4P 2Y3 (a division of Pearson Penguin
Canada Inc.) / Penguin Books Ltd, 80 Strand, London WC2R 0RL, England / Penguin Ireland, 25 St Stephen's Green, Dublin 2,
Ireland (a division of Penguin Books Ltd) / Penguin Group (Australia), 250 Camberwell Road, Camberwell, Victoria 3124,
Australia (a division of Pearson Australia Group Pty Ltd) / Penguin Books India Pvt Ltd, 11 Community Centre, Panchsheel Park,
New Delhi - 110 017, India / Penguin Group (NZ), Cnr Airborne and Rosedale Roads, Albany, Auckland 1310, New Zealand
(a division of Pearson New Zealand Ltd) / Penguin Books (South Africa) (Pty) Ltd, 24 Sturdee Avenue, Rosebank, Johannesburg
2196, South Africa / Penguin Books Ltd, Registered Offices: 80 Strand, London WC2R 0RL, England

LIBRARY OF CONGRESS CATALOGING-IN-PUBLICATION DATA

Compestine, Ying Chang.
The real story of stone soup / by Ying Chang Compestine ; illustrated by Stéphane Jorisch.—1st ed.
p. cm.
Summary: When some Chinese fishermen forget to bring cooking utensils with them,
they find creative ways to make do with what they have and what they can find.
ISBN 978-0-525-47493-7 (alk. paper)
[1. Folklore—China.] I. Jorisch, Stéphane, ill. II. Stone soup. English. III. Title.
PZ8.1.C73525Re 2007   398.2—dc22   [E]   2006014501

Published in the United States by Dutton Children's Books,
a division of Penguin Young Readers Group
345 Hudson Street, New York, New York 10014
www.penguin.com/youngreaders

Designed by Heather Wood
Manufactured in China / First Edition / 10 9 8 7 6 5 4 3 2

A NOTE FROM THE AUTHOR

In southeast China, there is a region called Xi Shuang Ban Na. Many minority tribes reside there. One tribe is famous for its stone soup. According to legend, fishermen first created stone soup. One day they forgot to bring cooking utensils with them. At mealtime, they started a fire to heat up some river stones, then dug a hole on the riverbank. They lined the hole with layers of plantain and banana leaves and filled the hole with river water. They dropped the hot river rocks from the fire into the soup to bring the soup to a boil.

They added in whatever food they had— fish they had caught that day, a few eggs they'd found in birds' nests, and fresh wild vegetables they'd harvested from the nearby hills. Finally, they seasoned the soup with salt, pepper, and sesame oil.

Since then stone soup has become a traditional dish in that area. It is famous for its unique fragrance and fresh taste brought out by the river stones. During my visit there, I ate many kinds of stone soup, including my favorite—Egg Drop Stone Soup.

$\mathcal{B}$y now, you have probably heard the old folktale about stone soup. A hungry soldier tricks some stingy villagers into making him a big pot of soup. The truth is that stone soup was invented here in China, and without any sly tricks.

Here is the real story.

It all began when I hired those troublesome Chang brothers to help me on my fishing boat. Nice boys, but lazy and, I'm sorry to say, somewhat stupid. The only good thing is I could get away with not paying them very much.

Even with three of them, I did most of the work, and I kept the hardest
job for myself. I steered the boat.

One summer day, after a full morning of fishing, I decided to stop early
for lunch.
"Time to eat, boys!" I yelled. "Dock the boat."

After the Chang brothers got the boat tied up, my work really began. Those boys were too dull to know what to do. "Ting! Gather firewood. Pong! Prepare the cooking pot and clean the fish. Kuai! Get some fresh water."

"The cooking pot isn't here," interrupted Ting, the oldest, a troublemaker. He always talked back to his elders.

"What do you mean the pot isn't here? Where is it?"

They looked at one another and shrugged.

"You boys forgot the cooking pot? How could you?" I asked.

"It's your pot," said Ting. "You should have remembered to bring it."

Those stupid potato heads! What were we to do now? Pong, the middle one and the most well-mannered of the three, tried to apologize. "Sorry, Uncle. We left in a hurry this morning, and we—"

Kuai, the youngest, interrupted. "We don't really need a pot to cook lunch." He whispered something to his brothers. Kuai is always full of silly ideas.

"How are we supposed to cook lunch?" I asked. "With a hole in the ground?"

Those crazy boys must have thought I meant it. No sooner had those words left my mouth than they started digging a hole in the sandy beach.

"What are you doing?" I asked.

"Cooking lunch, of course," said Kuai. He began to line the hole with banana leaves. Meanwhile, Ting and Pong started a huge fire next to the hole.

"Now we need some stones," said Kuai.

"For what?" I asked.

Kuai didn't answer. He picked up a nearby rock and held it to his ear. "This is a fish stone," he announced. Then he threw the rock in the fire.

"Come now," I said. "Even you can't be foolish enough to believe—"

"Shh!" Ting interrupted, holding a stone to his ear. "I need to hear what it is telling me. Aha! This is a fine vegetable stone." He tossed his rock into the fire, too.

I tried listening to a couple of stones. I didn't hear a thing. The hunger must have gone to their heads. "If you're so clever, what kind is this?" I handed a stone to Pong. He listened for a moment.

"Aha! Uncle, you are brilliant. You picked out a yummy egg stone." He pitched my stone into the fire.

I had no idea what he was blabbering about. But by this time I was hungry enough to eat anything, even stones.

"We need something to carry water from the river and to eat the soup with," said Kuai.

"Oh, Uncle," said Pong. "Could you use your mighty ax to make some bowls from bamboo stalks?"

"*Ai yo!*" I grumbled. "I have to do all the work, as always!" But it was true that none of them could be trusted with my sharp ax.

With a few quick chops, I made four bowls from a thick stalk. The boys used them to fill the hole with water.

I shook my head at them. "Now we have a puddle and a fire. How do you expect to get the water over the fire?" I asked. "Leave that to us," said Ting.

"Uncle, you made the best bowls in the village with nothing more than an ax," said Pong. "Could you use your graceful knife to make some chopsticks to go with them?"

"*Ai yo!*" I cried. "You lazy boys want me to do all the work." Nevertheless, I carved out some chopsticks. Unlike the Chang brothers, I wasn't stupid enough to eat hot stones with my fingers.

When I finished, I gave each boy a pair of my skillfully carved chopsticks. "How long does it take the stones to cook?" I worried that the stones might burn like potatoes. Then I couldn't believe what those crazy boys did next. With long sticks, Ting picked a stone out of the hot fire, and instead of offering it to his elder first, he held it before Kuai and Pong!

They didn't eat it, though. They whispered to it, *"Yú, yú, yú"* ("Fish, fish, fish"), and blew on it.

Then Ting dropped the stone into the hole. *Sploosh!*

"Ai yo!" I yelled.

Bubbles of steam shot off the stone as it sank to the bottom. The steam carried a wonderful fish smell. I saw pieces of fish floating in the soup. Those boys had told the truth—it really was a fish stone! My stomach purred like a kitten.

Kuai gently stirred the soup. "Hmm, this is turning into a tasty soup. If only we had a little salt, it would be a soup fit for a schoolmaster."

"Ting!" I said. "Get the salt off the boat."

"It's your salt. You get it," Ting said rudely. I was too hungry to teach him good manners. So I went to get the salt.

As I returned with the salt, Ting picked up the second stone and held it before his brothers. "*Cài, cài, cài.*" They whispered the word for vegetables three times and blew on the stone. Ting dropped it into the soup.

Shoosh! More steam leapt into the air. Surprisingly, I smelled vegetables! The aroma was so yummy, my stomach growled like an angry tiger.

Kuai stirred the soup again and sprinkled in a little salt. "This is a wonderful vegetable stone. If only we had a little sesame oil, this would be a soup fit for an emperor," said Kuai.

"Just a moment!" I cried. "I'll be right back with the sesame oil."

When I returned with the sesame oil, Ting was holding up the last stone. All three boys yelled, *"Dàn, dàn, dàn!"* ("Egg, egg, egg!") Then they each blew hard on the stone, one at a time.

"Why are you shouting at that stone, you potato heads?" I asked.

"Egg stones don't hear very well," said Ting. He dropped the stone into the soup.

Shoom! The hot stone brought the soup to a wild boil. I couldn't believe it when I saw threads of egg float to the top. A luscious fragrance filled the air. Even the monkeys came closer to get a whiff.

Kuai drizzled in the sesame oil. More delectable smells! By now I was sure the sounds from my hungry stomach could be heard back in the village.

Finally, Ting did something right. He filled one of the bamboo bowls with soup and served me, his elder, first.

I could hardly wait to taste it. I lifted the steaming bowl to my
lips and took a sip. "Mmmmm . . . *Hǎo chī! Hǎo chī!*" ("Tastes
good! Tastes good!") I must tell you that I have never tasted
such a wonderful soup! The fish from the fish stone
was tender and fresh. The wild
mushrooms and onions from
the vegetable stone were
flavorful. The threads
of egg from the
egg stone were
cooked just right.

Thanks to the bowls and chopsticks I had made, now the boys could
enjoy the soup, too. The rest of the afternoon, they were happy and even
worked a little harder. Not harder than me, of course.

From that day on, I always carried rocks in my pockets and told everyone the secret of making stone soup. I even demonstrated how to whisper to fish and vegetable stones, and how to yell at egg stones. But the truth is, I still haven't had time to make it. You know, I work too hard already.

And that, my friends, is how I invented the *real* stone soup. I don't know how people ended up with that silly old folktale.

CHANG BROTHERS' EGG DROP STONE SOUP

*This is how the Chang brothers would have cooked their soup
if they hadn't forgotten their cooking pot.*

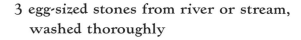

2 tablespoons canola oil

2 cloves garlic, finely chopped

¼ cup chopped onion

¼ cup fresh mushrooms

4 pieces of 4" x 4" banana leaf or grape leaf

2 medium tomatoes, cut into 2-inch cubes

1 pkg. (1.23 oz.) Hot & Sour Soup Mix
   or 4 cups chicken or vegetable broth

3 egg-sized stones from river or stream,
   washed thoroughly

8-ounce white fish fillet, such as catfish or halibut,
   cut into 2-inch chunks

1 large egg, well beaten

1 teaspoon sesame oil

1 tablespoon soy sauce

fresh cilantro leaves (optional)

Heat canola oil in large wok or skillet over medium-high heat. Add garlic, onion, mushrooms. Cook, stirring constantly, for about 1 minute or until fragrant. Add banana leaf or grape leaf and tomatoes; reduce heat to medium-low. Cook, stirring frequently, for 2 minutes.

Stir in soup mix and 4 cups water. *Add stones.* Bring to a boil. Add fish; bring to a second boil. Turn off heat. Stir soup in one direction with a chopstick or fork and slowly pour in the beaten egg so the egg forms long threads.

Stir in sesame oil and soy sauce. Garnish with cilantro leaves. Serve hot.

Note: Banana leaves evoke the flavor and aroma of the soup I had in Xi Shuang Ban Na. They are available in ethnic stores and ethnic sections in big supermarkets.